Tales of my Grandmother's
DREAMTIME
By NAIURA

BARTEL
PUBLICATIONS

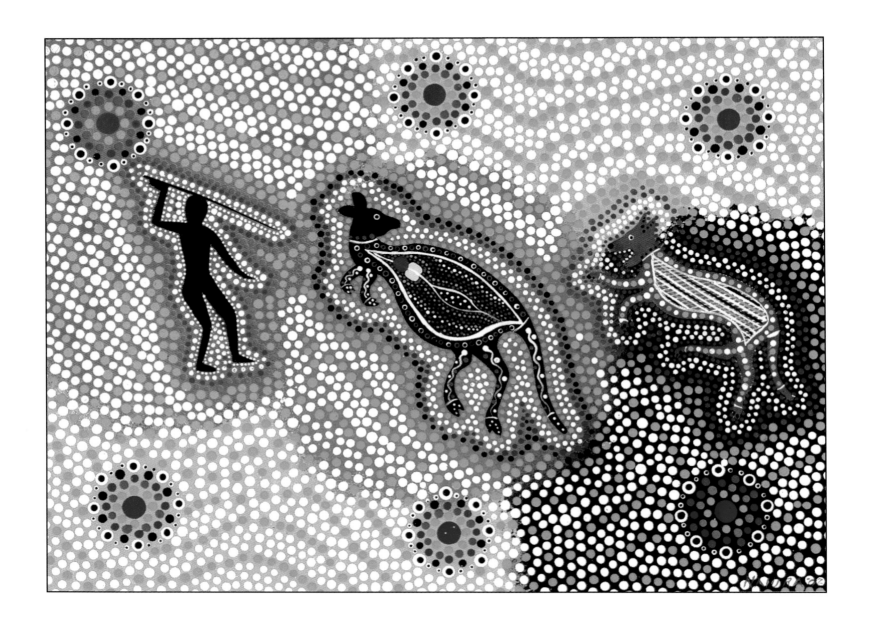

DREAMTIME SYMBOLS
THEIR MEANINGS

ABORIGINAL ART may be of a spiritual nature, or a record of a tribal event, or a personal experience. It is expressed in painting, carving or chiselling, on whatever media is available. It can be as simple as hands stencilled on a rock face, a sign that records someone was once there – that they existed. If Aboriginal art was traditionally portrayed in the abstract, usually by untrained hands, today's graduates of Aboriginal art schools produce a variety of work using modern media techniques, yet retaining a sense of Aboriginality. Even so, traditional Aboriginal art remains readily available for purists. Some works have brief story-lines, others are left to the imagination. Here is a readers' guide to symbols that are used to illustrate the Dreaming. Though helpful when reading this book, it should not be considered comprehensive nor absolute because various tribal interpretations, or an individual's expression, are not rigidly bound.

Camp site or water hole		Windbreak
Boomerang or clouds		Bushfire
Man sitting		Digging stick
Woman sitting		Shield
River, creek etc		Hands (action)
Spear		Eggs
Dish		Animal tracks:
Spear thrower		Kangaroo
Track, path		Emu
Man's footprints		Dingo
Woman's footprints		Goanna
Smoke or lightning		Snake
Ants		Rain

Published by Bartel Publications,
36 Rickety Street, Mascot,
NSW 2020, Australia

First published 2002, reprinted 2003, 2005, 2006, 2008, 2010

© copyright text and art by Nauira, 2002

Designed by Phillip Mathews Book Publishers

Printed by Tara TPS

ISBN 1-876206-19-5

CONTENTS

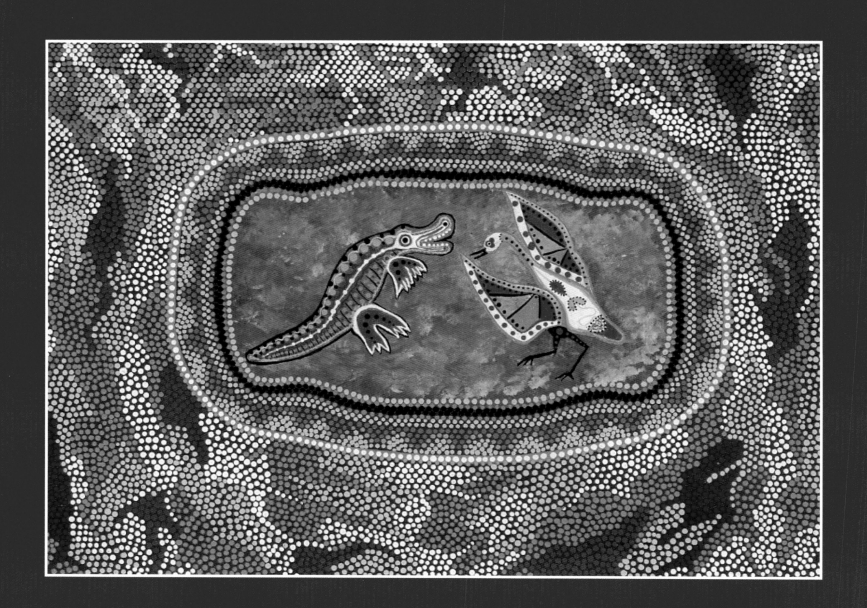

BARALGA
THE FOOLISH BROLGA

ARALGA the brolga was entranced as he watched the adult brolgas dance their graceful courting displays. How he longed to dance so precisely, so beautifully.

One day, when he felt sure he was alone by the river, he tried to dance himself. Spreading his splendid wings, he leaped from the ground in short, sharp steps. It started well; then his long legs began to wobble; then he tripped and fell. He tried again and again, but after a few promising steps he wobbled, then tripped, every time.

"It's no use," cried Baralga, stopping yet again to steady himself, "I shall have to wait till I grow a bit."

From shallows near the river bank, Kurria the crocodile raised his head and watched Baralga, hungrily. If he would only stray closer, mused Kurria, I might eat him.

"You dance so well," called Kurria slyly.

"How kind you are," replied Baralga , "but you wouldn't think so if you had seen the older birds."

"Oh, but I have," said Kurria. "They dance very well, I grant you, but no better than you." Kurria watched to see what effect his words had on the young brolga.

"You really think I'm good?" asked Baralga.

"Oh, yes." said Kurria. "I wish I could dance so well," he added, and Baralga was so pleased his chest swelled.

"Actually, this is only my first attempt to dance," said

Baralga, his shyness giving way to a little boasting.

Kurria saw that his flattery was working, and pressed his advantage.

"Well," he said, "I would never have believed that had you not told me."

"It's true," said Baralga, who felt unusually warm inside. No one had praised him before, for anything, and he liked it so much he wanted more.

"Shall I dance again," he offered, preening his feathers.

"Oh, please do," said Kurria, "I would like that very much indeed."

Baralga spread his fine wings and leaped into the air as he had done before (and wobbled as he had before). In fact, so eagerly did he flap and strut that even when he had to stop for a rest he remained excited. Vanity had quite got the better of him.

"There, what did you think of that?" he called.

"I am sure it was very good," said Kurria, "but you are so far away that I couldn't see you properly."

"Then I'll come closer," said Baralga, prancing and strutting in his very best brolga steps to the river bank, as Kurria had hoped. When Baralga was close enough, Kurria leapt from the water and grabbed him.

"What a foolish young bird," murmured Kurria as he sank beneath the water again, brolga feathers in his jaws.

DAYA-MINYA
REVEALS A TREE SPIRIT

E had hunted far in search of kooka, or meat, but by late morning of the fourth day, Wogalyu had found none. Tired and hungry, he rested in the shade of an ironbark tree at the edge of the forest.

Why had he not been rewarded, wondered Wogalyu. He had found barely enough food to keep hunting, though he had searched without pause. Yet he must keep going, he thought wearily. His family depended on him to eat.

"Where else can I look?" he sighed, "I can think of no other place."

"I will show you." said a voice, a voice as soft as he had ever heard.

Wogalyu looked about him. There, lying along a branch above, was the most beautifully coloured daya-minya—a small carpet python—he had ever seen. The snake held him steadily in its gaze as it slithered silently from the tree. When it reached the ground it turned and slid into the forest.

Wogalyu did not hesitate and rose quickly to follow. The daya-minya led him to a dead tree, where it stopped near a hollow in the trunk. There, it raised its head and began to sway very slowly from side to side.

His curiosity aroused, Wogalyu selected a long stick and poked it into the hollow. When he felt something soft, he twisted the stick sharply, so that it caught what was in there. When he pulled the stick out again he had a moodai, a possum, on the end of it.

Wogalyu stuffed it gratefully into his dilli bag and thanked the daya-minya. He was about to leave when the python spoke again, in a voice so hushed it was barely a whisper.

"Come!" it said, slithering deeper into the forest.

Again Wogalyu followed till it stopped in front of a large rock. The daya-minya raised its head over a small opening at the foot of the rock, and again it began to sway.

Wogalyu took a digging stick from his dilli and scraped away deep inside the shaded opening. In no time at all he had added a fat googarh, a goanna, to his catch.

With food for his family at last, Wogalyu felt relieved and grateful as he started the long journey home. The beautiful daya-minya, he now realised, was a Minggah, a tree spirit. It had taken the form of a python to help him.

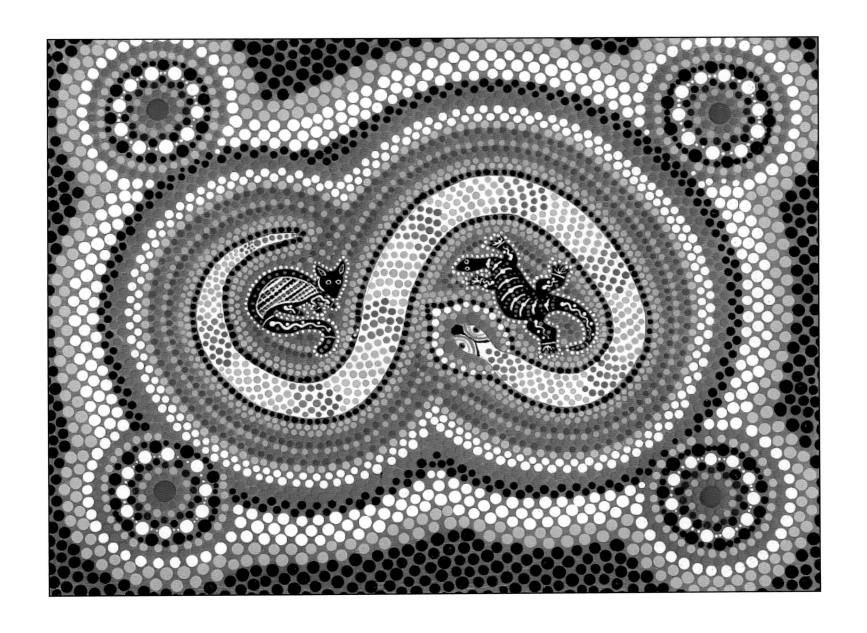

MOOROOP BINDAR
THE SPIRIT KANGAROO

HE tribal elders were anxious. Other tribes were hunting on their land without permission, causing great hardship for their tribe, the rightful owners.

At first, when it had been only one neighbouring tribe, they had ignored such bad manners because there had been more than enough animals to feed both tribes.

But soon other tribes, realising how peaceful the land-owners were, began to hunt there. This growing problem came to a head for the rightful landowners when the Mallee tribe crossed their borders. They treated the land as if it was their own, even making a camp there! Feared troublemakers, the Mallees not only caught more animals than they could eat, but fought with anyone who dared argue.

The animals on the land grew so wary that they went to ground. Some disappeared completely. This so concerned the tribal elders, who were afraid of the Mallees, that they decided a corroboree ceremony was their only hope. They would appeal to Baiame, The Great Spirit, for help.

Baiame heard their song and decided to help the fright-ened landowners, because there was no excuse for anyone to enter another tribe's land uninvited. Every tribe knew its own towri, or boundaries. To enter without permission ignored all their elders had taught them. A lesson was needed.

Days later, four Mallee mundurras, or hunters, who were camped inside their neighbour's boundary, set out to hunt.

When they spotted a big red kangaroo, a bindar, they approached from upwind so that it might not smell them, though the bindar grazed so openly that the mundurras felt little need for stealth. When they were close enough to spear it, the kangaroo turned. Instead of fleeing, the big red bindar simply rose to its full height and glared at them.

The mundurras were amazed. Why did it not flee? Was it blind? How fortunate, they thought, for the kill to be so easy. Rising boldly from their cover, the Mallee mundurras hurled their turas (spears). Yet the bindar remained unafraid and the spears bounced harmlessly off its body.

It was at that moment that the bindar chose to reveal itself as Baiame, The Great Spirit, and the Mallee mundurras were rooted to the spot in terror.

In fact, they never moved again, though their descendents can be seen to this day. They are the trees of the Mallee forest.

BARMINJARIN
THE GREEDY HUNTER

BARMINJARIN was a very fine hunter. So skilful was he that the tribe came to rely on him, trusting him to find food for them.

So rarely had he failed, Barminjarin grew anxious when he wandered far one day without finding game. When he had still found nothing by sunset, he camped. If he was patient, he thought, then tomorrow would be better.

Yet when he hunted again, the next day, he still found no meat. So again he camped, and tried the following day, but still without success. He hunted for seven days, but each day returned empty-handed.

By late afternoon of the seventh day Barminjarin had grown very hungry himself. Apart from a few berries, he had eaten nothing. As darkness fell, he decided to try one last time at a nearby billabong. Perhaps an unwary animal might water there.

When he approached the billabong, spear raised, he found only a few noisy galahs drinking — then silence.

Barminjarin glanced hungrily at some floating waterlilies. He could eat the lily bulbs but there were too few to feed him, let alone his people. There were fish, too, but much too small for a meal.

Famished, Barminjarin was about to return to camp when he spotted a honeycomb. It was so big, and so dripping with honey, that it could have fed his whole tribe. Barminjarin was so hungry, however, that he ate it all.

Just as he finished a spirit appeared, a spirit that took the form of one of his people.

"Why did you eat our honey?" asked the spirit.

"I didn't eat your honey," replied Barminjarin.

"Yes you did," said the spirit, "I saw you swallow every last mouthful!"

Realising he had been caught, Barminjarin confessed.

"First you stole our honey," said the spirit angrily, "then you lied. Why did you do that?"

"But I was so hungry," whined Barminjarin.

"If you're so hungry that you can ignore your tribe, then I shall take you to a place where there is plenty of food," said the spirit, leading Barminjarin to a tree. Pointing to a pile of stones at the base of the tree, the spirit said:

"There is the food you deserve."

When Barminjarin looked, he saw not stones but witchetty grubs. He greedily swallowed the lot, then fell to the ground as if dead. The spirit had not finished with him yet, however, because it turned Barminjarin, filled with the stones, into a star, a very lonely star.

BANJORA & UWAPPA
AND THE MUNDURRAS

ANJORA, the koala, who had never wandered off alone before, decided to explore. Climbing from one strange new branch to another, he strayed so far from his mother that he became lost.

Bewildered, he searched anxiously about him. Which way had he come? He could not recognise a single branch, let alone the tree, no matter how hard he looked. Banjora had not yet learned that everything looks different when viewed from a new direction, especially trees.

How Banjora longed for his mother to call out. Indeed, he was about to call himself, but a curious noise made him hesitate. When he looked down from his branch, his heart leapt with fear. Camped at the foot of the tree were two mundurras—hunters!

No wonder his mother had not called, he thought. The slightest sound could betray their presence to the mundurras. Banjora remained perfectly still, as his mother had taught him, yet so frightened he could hardly breathe.

Even when Banjora grew hungry, he dared not move in case the mundurras spotted him, though there were tasty gum leaves within reach. Nor could he retrace his steps because he did not know the way. Frightened and lonely, he wished he had not wandered so far from home.

Uwappa, the spider, who had been watching Banjora's plight, crawled across to the little koala.

"Stay still, Banjora, I shall hide you," whispered Uwappa.

"But how can someone so small hide me?" Banjora whispered back.

"You shall see," said Uwappa.

Uwappa began to weave a web, swinging and dangling, and swinging again, anchoring silky threads between branches. After he had woven a large silken frame, Uwappa spun a fine curtain of silk across it, working without pause. When at last the web was finished, it completely hid Banjora from the mundurras.

Banjora's mother, who had watched Uwappa weave the web from a distance, climbed quickly to Banjora.

"Oh, thank you Uwappa," she said, "the mundurras would have caught Banjora without your help."

"But I repay your kindness," said Uwappa. "How often have you let me snuggle into your fur to travel distances I could never have managed on my own?"

"Well, yes, but..." the mother's voice trailed off shyly.

Banjora clambered eagerly on to his mother's back, clinging tightly to her fur as she climbed towards the safety of their home. So carefully and so quietly did she climb, that the mundurras never knew koalas had ever been there.

The mundurras noticed Uwappa's new web, of course, but ignored it. Of what interest could a spider web be to a mundurra? They were hunting for meat, after all.

DINEWAN, BINDAR & GOOGARH
A COLOURFUL WISH

DINEWAN the emu watched his reflection in the billabong and sighed. His feathers looked so drab. Why, he wondered moodily, was he not colourful like other birds.

Then Dinewan had an idea. Gathering every bright feather and flower petal he could find, he tucked them into his feathers. When completely covered, he rushed back to the billabong to see how it looked. There, in his reflection, was the most beautiful, colourful bird he had ever seen.

Dinewan, who could not wait to show off his radiant new colours, was strutting across the plain when Bindar, the kangaroo, spotted him.

"What beautiful bird is this?" gasped Bindar.

"Don't you recognise me Bindar? It is I, Dinewan."

"But you look so colourful," said Bindar. "How did you do that?"

Dinewan explained how and urged Bindar try. They were soon searching together for more feathers and petals when Googarh, the goanna, approached.

"What are you doing?" he asked.

"Making ourselves beautiful," said Bindar. "Why don't you join us?"

Dinewan, Bindar and Googarh were already quite colourful when Yurlunggur, the Rainbow Snake appeared.

"Why do you adorn yourselves so?" asked Yurlunggur.

"To make us beautiful, like birds and flowers," they said.

"But why don't you like the colours I gave you?" said Yurlunggur.

"Oh, they are much too drab." said Bindar.

"Foolish creatures!" said Yurlunggur. "I gave you special colours to help you blend with the bush, to make you hard to find. Those who cannot see you, cannot eat you."

"But other birds have beautiful colours," said Dinewan.

"Only if they feed among the trees and bushes and the wildflowers of the plains." said Yurlunggur. "Bright colours suit their needs, just as drab colours suit yours'."

Yurlunggur stared steadily at each animal but they remained unmoved. They wanted bright colours!

"Well, if that is what you really want, then so be it," he said sadly. He circled the animals several times, and their drab natural covering suddenly burst into vivid colours.

Overjoyed, the three animals dashed off across the plain together, eager to display their new finery.

They were spotted, almost at once. A party of mundurras, or hunters, could hardly miss them.

"What strange and beautiful creatures," said one.

"Oh, yes," chuckled another, "and if they taste as good as they look, what a feast we shall have!"

And a very fine feast it was.

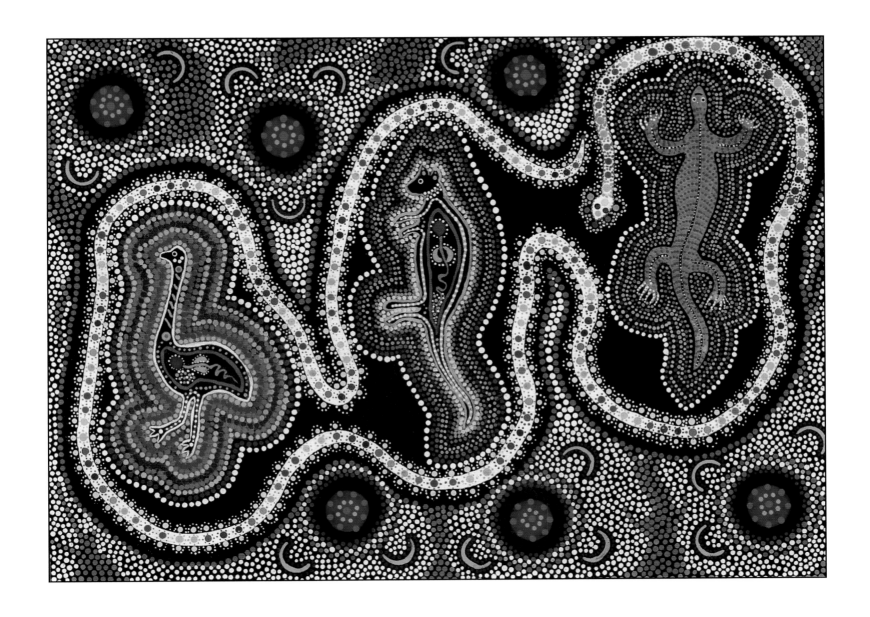

YARRAWAH-WILYANGO
THE STORM BOY

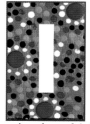T had not rained for so many months that the creeks and billabongs were drying. Even the scrub withered under the burning sun. The animals, which had fled their usual feeding grounds as the drought took hold, forced the mundurras, or hunters, to search for days to find food.

In time, the drought grew so serious that the tribal elders decided that only a corroboree ceremony could help. They would appeal to the rain spirits to bring mokra—rain!

Musicians gathered around the campfires for the ceremony, as did the dancers, their bodies decorated with white clay markings. Then the wirrinun, a wise man, took his position in the ceremonial clearing. When he nodded to the musicians, the corroboree began.

The men danced well into the night without a sign of success. There was no hint of rain, but still they danced. There could be no stopping.

Beyond the glow of the corroboree, the women stood with their children. Among these was a small boy, or wilyango, who could contain himself no longer.

"They should sing much louder and dance harder!" he blurted out.

"Be silent," hissed his mother. "Only a wirrinun is wise enough to know what is needed."

The boy continued to gaze towards the corroboree. If the dancers made more effort, he thought stubbornly, it would surely rain. Then, before his mother could stop him, he dashed from her side into the lighted circle.

He began to sing and dance.

So loud did he sing and so wildly did he dance that the other performers stopped, then stared in disbelief. The small boy waved his hands and stamped his feet so hard that he could barely be seen through the cloud of dust he raised.

Suddenly a bolt of lightning—doongarra—crackled across the night sky. A great clap of dooloomal, or thunder, followed. Then the dark skies opened. Rain fell in such torrents that the ground was soon awash, rushing into foaming creeks to fill the dry billabongs.

The little boy stared at the storm, frightened by its terrible force.

"I'm sorry," he wailed, "I hadn't meant it to rain this hard."

The men exchanged glances, then chuckled softly at such cheek. The boy had been very naughty, but they realised he had only meant to help. What harm could there be, they reasoned, if just this once they let him believe that his dance alone had brought such a deluge.

Nor were his efforts forgotten, because the small boy was known always as Yarrawah-Wilyango, the Storm Boy.

MARLOO'S GREAT LEAP
AND KURRIA'S CUNNING TRAP

 ARLOO, the young red kangaroo, stared across the swollen river to the opposite bank. It had rained heavily, and the river was flowing faster, darker, and wider than it had been when he jumped across it a day earlier.

"I wonder," he muttered, "could I still jump it?"

"Well, with such long legs, I believe you could," said an encouraging voice below him. It was Googarh, the goanna.

"It's a very long way," said Marloo doubtfully.

"Of course you should jump," called Kurria, the crocodile. "It's not far at all."

Kurria had risen silently to the surface, only his eyes showing. They seemed to rest on the water.

This troubled Marloo even more as he looked across.

"But if I land in the water you will eat me," said Marloo, shaking his head.

"Oh, no," said Kurria, "I would never do that."

"Oh yes you would," shouted Marloo and Googarh.

"All right," said Kurria, "what if I lay on the very bottom of the river? Would that convince you?"

Marloo thought quickly, perhaps too quickly.

"All right," he said. "Down you go."

Kurria slowly sank, but not to the bottom of the river as he had promised. He lay just below the dark surface, waiting in ambush.

Marloo shuffled a long way back from the riverbank, paused, then bounded forward, hopping faster and faster, till a breeze whistled along his furry flanks. When he reached the water's edge, he sprang as high and far as he could, soaring towards the opposite bank, trailing his powerful legs behind him for better distance.

"You're going to make it!" shouted Googarh.

"No he isn't!" snarled Kurria, who leapt from the water, jaws gaping.

Marloo was wide-eyed when he realised he was falling short, towards the greedy jaws. Then, as Kurria was about to snap them shut, Marloo wrenched his hind legs forward hard, rapping the crocodile's snout. The kangaroo's strong legs struck Kurria's tough snout so hard that he bounced off, just far enough to reach the safety of the bank.

Marloo had bounded off on his way when Kurria surfaced again. Only his eyes showed above the water, but this time they were smarting—and it didn't help that Googarh was chuckling to himself on the other bank.

THE NURUNDERI
AND THE KOOLYANGARRA

ELDOM were aged animals hunted, unless game was very, very scarce. Yet when confused old animals wandered into a camp, they were often teased by koolyangarra. These children pretended they were mundurras, or hunters, tormenting the old animals with blunted toy spears.

One day an aged mari, a wallaby, entered the baanya and began to graze. The koolyangarra quickly gave chase, but the mari nimbly avoided the blunted spears. In spite of his age, he even jumped over the heads of the koolyangarra, till the children grew angry.

"Keep still," they shouted. "We cannot 'kill' you if you jump about so."

The mari stopped and faced them.

"Why do you want to kill me?" he said.

The koolyangarra were spellbound.

"How can you speak like us?" they asked.

"To avoid being killed," said the mari.

"But you are a mari, and maris don't speak," said the koolyangarra.

"Is that so?" said the mari.

Then, to the children's astonishment, the mari turned into one of the spirit people. Finally the spirit spoke:

"I am a nurunderi, a spirit teacher, sent by The Great Spirit, Baiame. I come to teach you respect.

"How often have I seen you tease old animals. And how it displeases me! You should hunt only for food, never for fun. All creatures deserve dignity, because each has a purpose, even if that purpose is beyond the understanding of children. Above all, age should be respected, because with age there is wisdom, which is passed on to the young."

"We do respect the elders," said a wilyango, or boy. "But what can we learn from an old animal?"

"Were you able to catch the mari?" asked the nurunderi. "Or kill it?"

The boy shuffled and looked at his feet, feeling very foolish.

"You see," said the nurunderi, "age and experience teaches much." He paused for some time, then he added:

"Only if you remember these things can each of you one day become good mundurras, and if you do then your people will never go hungry."

The koolyangarra looked at each for only a moment, yet when they looked back the nurunderi had vanished

THE WILY GOOGARH
AND THE MUNDURRAS

OUR mundurras—hunters—crept towards the goanna with clubs raised. The googarh, who was sunning himself on a warm rock, seemed unaware of any danger. Big and fat, he would make a good meal.

In fact, the googarh had seen the mundurras but had decided to rely on his wits, because he was much too old to outrun them. He continued to sun himself, which pleased the mundurras. Just as they were about to leap on him, however, the googarh rose. He ran in a small circle, waving his legs about. Then he stopped. Then he did it again.

The mundurras were confused.

"What are you doing?" they asked.

"I am dancing," said the googarh.

"Be still for a moment, googarh, so we can kill you," they said impatiently.

"Why do you want to kill me?" asked the googarh.

"To cook you and eat you, of course" said the mundurras, who were starting to get angry.

"I see." said the googarh, unhappily. "Well, if this is to be my very last dance, would you promise not to kill me before I'm finished?"

The mundurras discussed this for some time. In the end they agreed it was only fair, so they made the promise.

"Thank you," said the googarh, who began to dance again. Indeed, he danced on and on, all through the day, then into the night. The mundurras, bound by their promise, were dismayed. As time passed they grew impatient. By nightfall they were quite angry.

"How much longer, googarh?" they demanded.

"My dance ends when the sun rises," said the googarh.

"But that's not till tomorrow," they howled.

"Perhaps you could come back then?" googarh suggested in a polite manner.

The mundurras laughed.

"We are not so foolish," they said. "If we left, you would stop dancing and run away."

The mundurras decided that each should make a separate camp. In this way they could surround the googarh. There could be no escape. They would wait and watch till the sun came up. Then they would eat him.

As each mundurra sat by his own fire, he grew warm and comfortable, then drowsy. One by one they fell asleep. Not wishing to disturb their peace, the googarh decided that his dance was now completed. Then the wily old goanna shuffle quietly away.

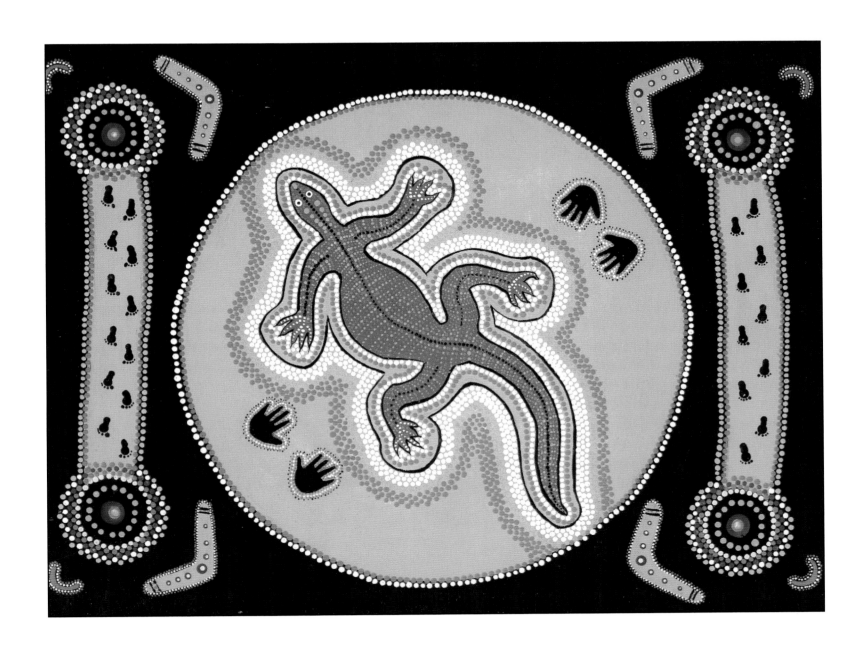

YANDARLANA BOLOKE
LAKE OF TEARS

URING the Dreamtime, a beautiful lake marked the border of several tribal lands. All the birds and animals, as well as the neighbouring tribes, went there to drink. The water was fresh and pure, and the fish were big. Even enemies could drink at the lake together. It was a sacred lake, placed there for all to share by Baiame, The Great Spirit.

One day, two tribes had an argument at the lake, though nobody ever discovered the reason. In the furious battle that followed, the lake turned red with kandara—blood!

Then something else happened that had never happened before. The lake dried up. All that remained of the once glittering waters was a big, dry bowl of red dust.

"Where has the water gone?" wailed the thirsty tribes.

When Baiame finally spoke, he was very angry.

"How ungrateful you are," he roared. "You have ruined the sacred lake for all and brought disgrace upon your tribes. You no longer deserve it."

"But where are we to get water?" they cried.

"You must find it," said Baiame, and then he was gone.

From that terrible moment, all the living creatures had to travel far and wide to search for water.

Many years later, a group of koolyangarra, or children, were playing in the red dust bowl. One explained to the others that his grandfather had told him that a beautiful lake once filled the very dust bowl in which they now played. This alone made the koolyangarra miserable, but when they realised how foolish their ancestors had been, the children grew even sadder.

They began to cry.

The wailing grew so loud that it attracted great numbers of birds and animals, who clustered round the dust bowl.

"Why do you cry, koolyangarra?" they called.

When the birds and animals heard the story, they too were miserable. Then, they too began to cry.

So sad were they all that they cried for days and days, the tears of all the children and all the birds and all the animals spilling on to the parched red dust.

Slowly, very slowly, a lake began to form.

When at last it was filled, the children ran to tell all the tribal elders, who came to see for themselves. Deep, glittering waters had returned to where only dust had been. All the birds and the animals and the people were happy again.

But their joy did not last. When they drank the water they became sad again. It tasted of tears, too salty to drink.

Ever since that day, the lake has always been known as Yandarlana Boloke, the Lake of Tears.

YURLUNGGUR IN ALCHERINGAH
THE RAINBOW SNAKE IN DREAMLAND

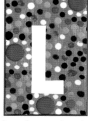ONG before there was a place where the old people lived, called Alchera, there was another place. This was called Alcheringa, the Dreamland, or the Land of Baiame.

Alcheringa was a desolate land, surrounded by water. No living thing existed there: neither people, nor animals, not even scrub. So still and silent was it that not a breeze stirred the dry dust.

"This will not do," said Yurlunggur, the Rainbow Snake.

He must, he decided, endow this miserable place with beauty. First, he filled the water with fishes. Then he covered the land with grasses and flowers, and trees that blossomed. Next, he made birds and animals to feed among them, and provided fresh water to drink.

Finally, Yurlunggur made people.

At first, the people wandered all over the land, taking all they wanted. In time, they took from each other, which caused squabbles. Soon after, the people began to fight with each other, causing kandara, or blood, to flow.

Yurlunggur was displeased. If things kept going as they were, he realised, there would soon be no people left. So he called all the people together.

From now on, Yurlunggur told them, all people would be divided into separate tribes, each with its own land, so that all tribes could live in peace with each other.

"How shall we know which land is ours?" the people asked him.

"I shall set boundaries for each tribe, called towri," said Yurlunggur, "and every tribe must respect them. No one may hunt on another tribe's lands without permission, or take anything from it."

To encourage the tribes, Yurlunggur gave each its own spirits. These spirits would watch over all members of the tribe, he said, but he added a warning:

"Stray over the towri into another's land, and you lose the protection of your own tribal spirits. You will find yourself not only homeless but defenceless; and exposed to the fury of the spirits that protect the tribal lands into which you have trespassed. Each must learn his own tribal towri."

From then on, tribal territories were strictly observed. The punishment was so severe that few dared hunt in another's lands without permission. Nor would they dare remove anything without consent, such at sticks for spears, stones for tools, or clays for ceremonial decoration. To enter the land of a neighbouring tribe—called a tauel—without asking became almost unthinkable.

In time, the tribes learnt that so long as Yurlunggur's words were respected, there would be peace between them.

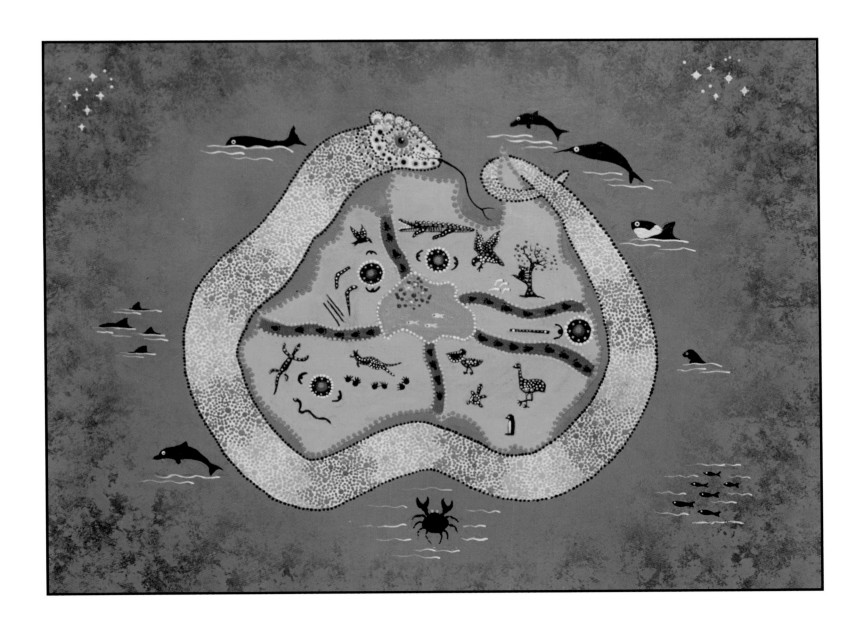

BULAROOL & THE BUNYIP
A TEST OF WISDOM

BULAROOL had hunted well that night. The wise old owl was quite full but now he needed a drink. He was about to fly down to the water's edge, when a sudden movement stopped him.

The dark waters swirled. Crocodile, thought Bularool, and remained in his tree. But when the waters swirled again, a huge creature broke the surface. It looked around for only a moment then clambered slowly on to the bank, between Bularool and the water.

Bularool was puzzled by its ugliness and frightened by its size. It was so big when it stood that its head reached almost as high as the old owl's perch. Then he knew.

It was a bunyip, the monster of the lake.

Bularool remained absolutely still, which made him almost invisible in the tree. The fright had made him even thirstier, but he knew the bunyip would eat him if he flew down to the water.

After a while, Bularool grew so thirsty that he realised he must risk his wits with the bunyip.

"Hello!" he called. "Bunyip!"

The bunyip looked about but could see no one.

"Who dares speak my name?" he demanded.

"I, Bularool," said the old owl.

The bunyip's huge eyes turned to the direction of the voice. It was some time before he spotted the old owl, so well did the darkened leaves conceal him.

"What are you doing up there, old owl?" asked the bunyip.

"I am waiting to get a drink," replied Bularool.

"Then fly down and get one," said the bunyip. "You'll be quite safe. I won't eat you."

Bularool was much too old and wise to trust a bunyip.

"I can't get down, Bunyip, because I dropped my wings in the lake. They sank all the way to the bottom," said Bularool, who knew the lake was very deep.

"That is a pity," said the bunyip, though he was thinking about the small meal that was just beyond his grasp.

"Would you be kind enough to get my wings for me, Bunyip?" asked Bularool.

The bunyip thought quickly. If he could not climb the tree to catch Bularool, perhaps he should get the wings so that old owl could fly down—for a small but tasty meal.

(The old owl was also thinking. The lake was so deep that even a bunyip would take time to reach the bottom, and then he would have to search for wings.)

"All right, I'll do it," said Bunyip slyly, and dived into the dark lake, swimming hard towards the bottom.

Bularool waited only a moment. Gliding down from his perch, he took a long, satisfying drink. Then he stretched his wings and flew off, a very wise old owl indeed.

THE PIGGI-BILLA

A GREEDY ECHIDNA

IGGI-BILLA, the echidna, was already very hungry when he spotted a tall termite mound. He needed enough food to fill him for the long journey home, and white ants were his favourite. He dug the mound open with his claws and scooped out the mirtas—the white ants—with his long sticky tongue. He was so hungry he did not stop till he had swallowed every mirta and mirta egg he could find. In fact, he ate so many mirtas that he grew too full to walk home. So he curled up beside the crumbled termite mound and soon dozed off.

An angry voice startled him. It was Googarh, the goanna.

"What do you think you are doing?" he shouted.

"I'm sleeping before going home," said Piggi-billa.

"Well, you can't," said Googarh. "That's my spot."

"Then I'll move," offered Piggi-billa.

"Not good enough," said Googarh, "because this is all my territory."

"I only need a little sleep," groaned Piggi-billa, his heavy stomach now aching.

"Very well," said Googarh, "but you must give something in return."

"But I have nothing to give," said Piggi-billa.

"You have your spines. I'll take them," said Googarh.

"No you can't," said Piggi-billa. "They protect me."

"Well, I need protection too," said Googarh.

"But you have thick, scaly skin and swift legs to protect you," said Piggi-billa.

"They're not enough when bilyara, the wedge-tail eagle, dives like lightning from the sky," replied Googarh.

"True," said Piggi-billa, "but you can't have my spines."

"Oh yes I will," said Googarh, picking up a muggil, a sharp stone used for cutting. "It won't take long if you keep still."

Piggi-billa ran for his life, scuttling away on his tiny legs. He was much too slow to outrun a goanna, of course, and even slower with a very full belly. Googarh followed him easily, cutting off spine after spine.

When Piggi-billa could run no more, he curled into a ball of bristling spines. This was his only defence, but it would not stop a muggil. He waited for the end, but nothing happened. He waited longer, but still nothing happened.

After a very long time, Piggi-billa uncurled himself just enough to peek out. He was still beside the termite mound but there was no Googarh, and no muggil in sight, and he still had all his spines.

It had all been a bad dream from eating too much. Piggi-billa would not be so greedy next time.

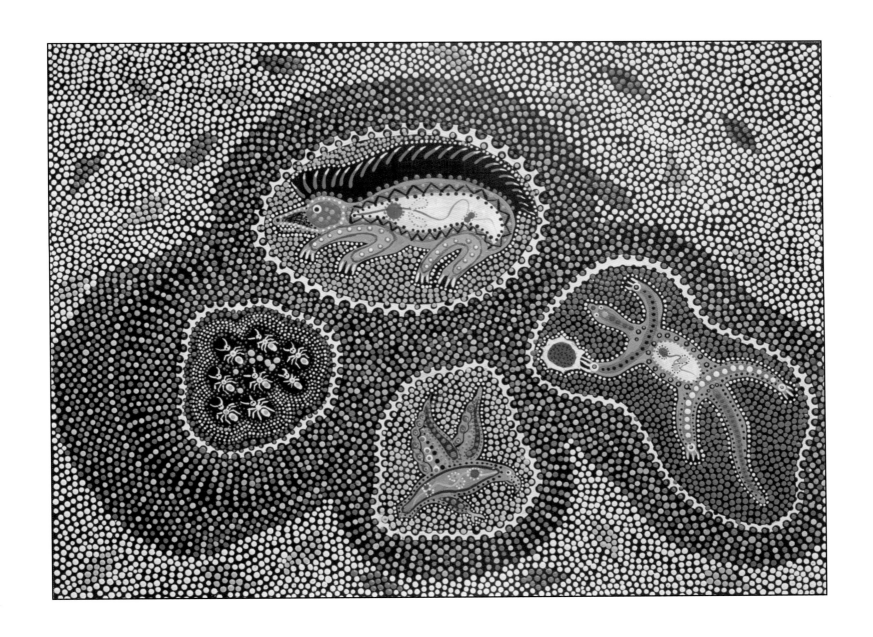

THE GUBBERA
THE STRANGE POWER OF MAGIC

INJARA felt ashamed as he returned from the hunting grounds. It was his first hunt since his bora, the tribal initiation ceremony that marked him as a man and a hunter. Yet he had caught nothing, nothing at all.

Why, he asked his father sadly, had he failed to bring back any kooka, or meat, from the hunt. He had tried as hard as he could, just as his uncles had taught him.

Binjara's father listened gravely before he spoke.

"Wait," he said, "because I have something that will help." When he returned, he handed Binjara a stone.

Binjara studied the stone.

"Is it a gubbera, a magic stone?" he whispered.

"Unlike any you will ever see," said his father.

Binjara did not hesitate. He placed the stone in his dilli bag, gathered his hunting weapons and left the baanya, the camp.

Later that day, Binjara spotted a mob of bindars—kangaroos—grazing. Hiding himself carefully upwind so that they did not catch his scent, he lay still for a long time, watching. When certain he had not disturbed them, he crept forward, crouching low in the scrub, his spear raised. When he was close enough, he hurled his spear.

A big bindar looked up too late. Binjara's aim was true and the kangaroo fell to the ground.

Binjara returned to his tribe, the big bindar across his young shoulders. This time, when he went to his father, he was pleased and a little proud.

"The gubbera is indeed magic," said Binjara. "I could never have got so close to the bindar without it. The stone made me invisible."

"The stone did nothing," said his father. "Nothing!"

"But you said it was a magic stone," said Binjara.

"I did not say it was magic," said his father, "I said it was unlike any gubbera you would ever see. And that is true, because it is nothing more than a very ordinary stone that I found on the plain."

Binjara was confused, so his father explained:

"You succeeded on your hunt because you believed the stone had magic. That belief gave you the self-confidence you needed to do well. Now that you have found it, your self-confidence is far more useful than any stone."

"Even a gubbera?" asked Binjara.

"More than a gubbera!" said his father.

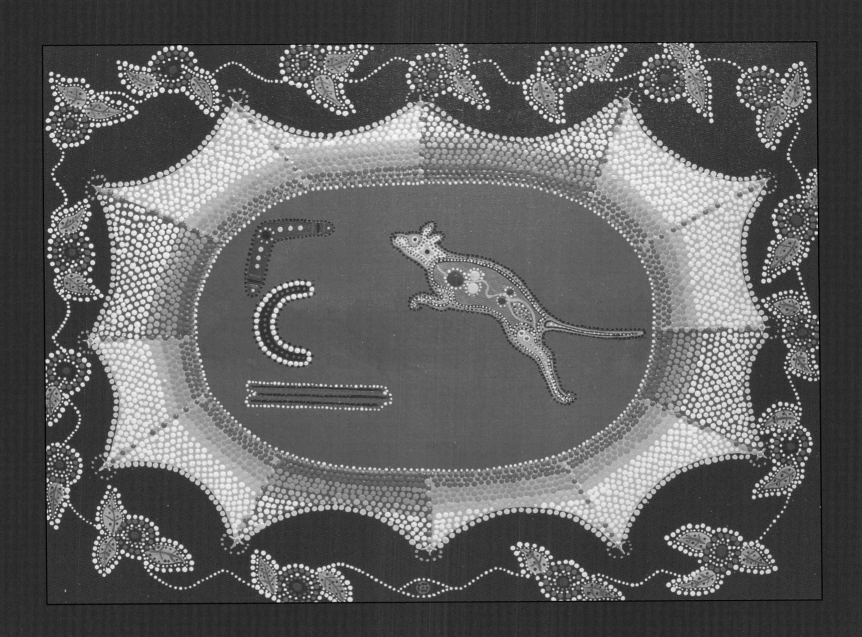

THE BOASTFUL DOLPHIN
WHO JUMPED TOO HIGH

HUKO, the sun, was up; warringah, the sea, was calm; and makora, the fish, were plentiful. The pod of dolphins, including adults and their young, were content.

A juvenile dolphin swam alongside a mother with a young one, and spoke to her offspring.

"If you come to the surface, young one, I will show you how high I jump," he said

"May I?", asked the young one, looking to his mother.

The mother hesitated. The juvenile could certainly leap high, possibly higher than any of them. Yet his boasting annoyed the other dolphins, because it never stopped.

"Very well," she said reluctantly.

"Come," said the juvenile. "You'll never believe how high I jump if you don't see it." He flipped his tail and sped towards the surface, followed closely by the young one.

"Leap the waves, young one, and I shall leap higher," he taunted. And he did so, very easily, and every time.

"Why do you boast so much?" asked the young one, who was otherwise very impressed. "You so clearly leap the highest that there is no need for you to say so?"

"Why not?" replied the juvenile, "when I am the best!"

"Then let others say so," said the young one.

"But they don't," said the juvenile, "because they're jealous."

"Perhaps they're just afraid of making you even more pleased with yourself," said the young one.

"Well, I don't care!" said the juvenile.

The two dolphins played happily together all day, but when the setting sun became a big red ball on the horizon, the young one turned back to find the pod.

The juvenile lingered.

"Just watch one last jump," he begged. "I shall jump right over the setting sun!"

"Don't be foolish. It's impossible!" said the young one.

The juvenile laughed as he sped towards the sun. When he reached the horizon, he exploded from the water in a towering leap, much higher than any dolphin had ever leapt; yet not quite as high as his boast. He disappeared into the blazing red sun, which swallowed him.

The young one felt miserable as he swam down to find his mother. His wonderful friend had leapt higher than any dolphin had ever dreamed of, yet he would never be able to boast about it. Not even once, because no one would ever hear him again.

WARRIGAL & THE MUNDURRA
THE OLD DINGO & THE HUNTER

 ARRIGAL, the old dingo, crept towards the black wallaby. Tired and hungry, he moved with great care, because he was much too old to run down the bunderra if it spotted him. He was almost within striking distance when the wallaby raised its head sharply, spun on its hind legs, and was gone.

Warrigal wondered what had startled the bunderra, so he kept low and watched. He did not have long to wait.

An old mundurra, a hunter, appeared out of the scrub. Warrigal growled angrily to himself, then sighed and decided to remain hidden till the old man had gone.

The old man was just as angry, because he too had been tracking the bunderra. He too was wondering what had startled it, when out of the corner of his eye he noticed the crouching Warrigal.

"You're not as good to eat as a bunderra," he muttered, "but I am so hungry that even a skinny warrigal will do."

When Warrigal saw the old mundurra raise his tura—his spear—he sprang to his feet and trotted away. The mundurra gave chase but the pace was slow. Neither was swift because of their age. Both were weary from hunger.

When Warrigal could run no further, he turned on the mundurra.

"Why do you chase me, old brother?" he panted.

The mundurra, who was also relieved to stop, stood over Warrigal with his spear still raised, though unsteadily.

"I want to kill you and eat you," he replied. "And you are not my brother," he added scornfully.

"Yet we are surely brothers of a sort," said Warrigal. "We are both lonely hunters, and our old age unites us more."

The old mundurra scratched his beard as he considered this. Then he rested his tura on the ground and sat down to get his breath back.

"Perhaps we are brothers, at least in spirit" he said.

"That's my point," said Warrigal. "So, what shall we do? Brothers may not kill each other, yet we both must eat."

"And neither of us eats well any more," grumbled the old mundurra, who was as thin and bony as the dingo.

Warrigal nodded and sighed, watching the old man closely. The mundurra sighed too, then scratched his beard again as he thought about their problem.

"If we are brothers," he said finally, "and perhaps we are, then we should hunt together, and share what we catch. We might both eat better together than separately."

And so they did. The old man and the old dingo hunted together, shared food and campfires together, and became close friends. So did all their descendants—men and dogs—who can be seen together in any baanya, or camp.

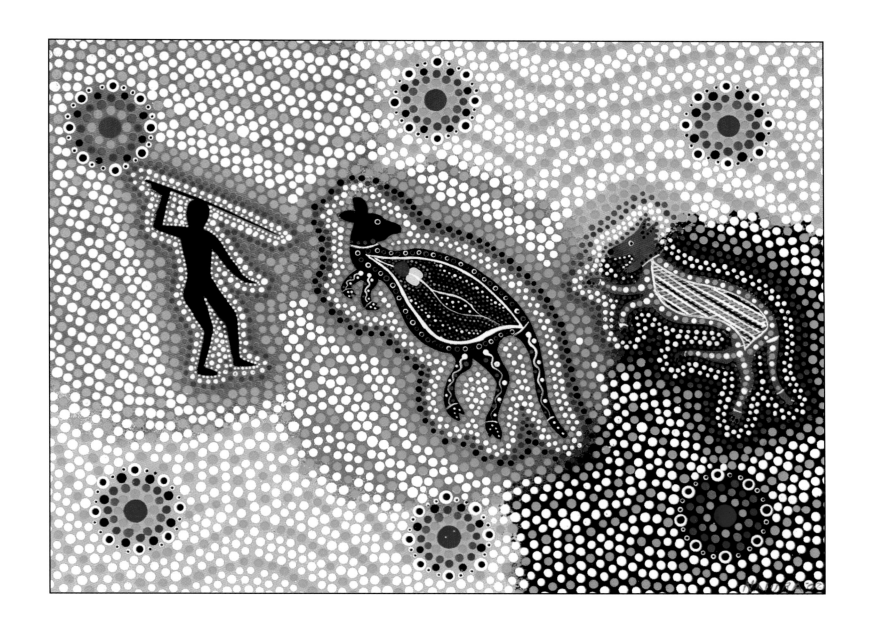